NORTH AMERICAN
ANIMALS

BIGHORN
SHEEP

by Jill Sherman

AMICUS | AMICUS INK

Amicus High Interest and Amicus Ink are imprints of Amicus
P.O. Box 1329, Mankato, MN 56002
www.amicuspublishing.us

Library of Congress Cataloging-in-Publication Data
Title: Bighorn sheep / by Jill Sherman.
Description: Mankato, MN : Amicus/Amicus Ink, [2019] | Series: North
 American animals | Audience: K to grade 3. | Includes bibliographical
 references and index.
Identifiers: LCCN 2017049956 (print) | LCCN 2017052369 (ebook) | ISBN
 9781681514970 (pdf) | ISBN 9781681514154 (library binding) | ISBN
 9781681523354 (pbk.)
Subjects: LCSH: Bighorn sheep--Juvenile literature. | Sheep--Juvenile
 literature.
Classification: LCC QL737.U53 (ebook) | LCC QL737.U53 S4827 2019
 (print) | DDC 599.649--dc23
LC record available at https://lccn.loc.gov/2017049956

Photo Credits: equigini/iStock cover; Robert Ingelhart/iStock 2; raincoast/
iStock 4–5; Brandon Smith/Alamy Stock Photo 7; iStock 8–9; Tom
Reichner/Shutterstock 10–11; Nick Trehearne/All Canada Photos/Alamy
Stock Photo 12; Donald M. Jones/Minden 14–15; Nick Trehearne/All
Canada Photos/AgeFotoStock 16–17; Sumio Harada/
Minden 18–19; Donald M. Jones/Minden 20–21;
gqxue/iStock 22

Editor: Wendy Dieker
Designer: Aubrey Harper
Photo Researcher: Holly Young

Printed in China

HC 10 9 8 7 6 5 4 3 2 1
PB 10 9 8 7 6 5 4 3 2 1

TABLE OF CONTENTS

BIG HORNS

Do you see that sheep with the big horns? It's a bighorn sheep! Males, or **rams**, have huge, curved horns. By age eight, the ram's horns curve around his face. Females, or **ewes**, have smaller horns.

MOUNTAIN CLIMBERS

These sheep jump and climb up cliffs in the Rocky Mountains of North America. Their **hooves** have rubber-like soles. They are like your sneakers! They help sheep grip the ground.

Check This Out
The outer part of the bighorn's hoof is hard. It is like a toenail.

OUT OF REACH

A bighorn spots a bear. The sheep races to higher ground. Up and up, the bighorn leaps. It goes up the cliff face. **Predators** don't climb as quickly. Bighorns find safety in the mountains.

Check This Out
Bears, coyotes, and mountain lions hunt bighorns.

EAT AND RUN

Bighorns come down to the grassy valleys to eat. They quickly chomp grass, seeds, and plants. When they have had their fill, they go back up the mountain. There they safely **digest** their food.

BACK TO BED

Bighorns are most active during the day. At night, they move back to flat spots on higher ground. They sleep there. Bighorns will use the same bed for many years.

HERD BEHAVIOR

Groups of bighorns are called **herds**. Living in a herd helps keep them safe. Rams live in one group. Ewes and lambs live in another. Rams and ewes come together for mating season.

LOCKING HORNS

Rams compete for **mates**. They face each other. They rear up. Then they race at each other. Crash! Their horns clack together. They go again. Crack! They fight until one ram walks away.

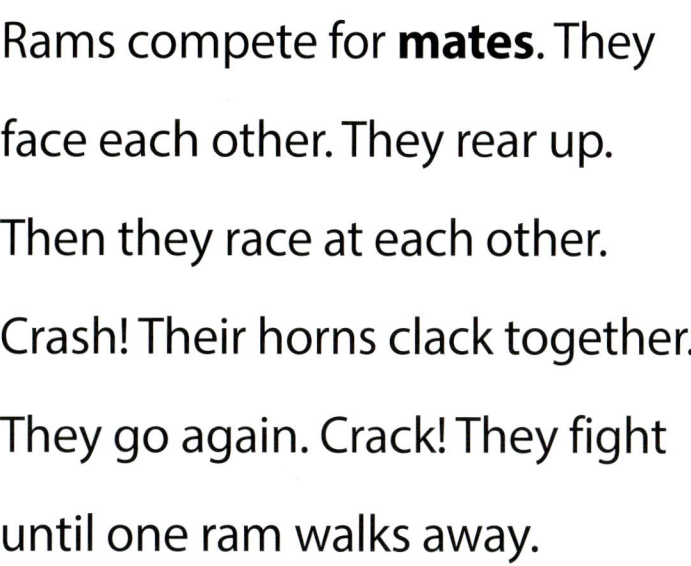

Check This Out

Rams may fight for hours. The clash of their horns echoes loudly.

OUT ON A LEDGE

Ewes give birth on mountain ledges. The lambs have little horn buds. Within a day, lambs can walk and climb as well as adults. Lambs stay with their mothers for their first few years.

SHEEP WATCHING

Bighorn sheep live in many protected parks. They can be hard to spot. Their gray and brown coats blend in with the landscape. Look for them on slopes and in valleys.

A LOOK AT BIGHORN SHEEP

curved horn

gray-brown fur

rubbery hoof

WORDS TO KNOW

digest – to break down food in the body.

ewe – a female bighorn sheep.

herd – a group of animals that lives and moves together.

hoof – a covering of horn that covers the toes of some mammals.

mate – one of a breeding animal pair.

predator – an animal that hunts other animals.

ram – a male bighorn sheep.

LEARN MORE

Books

Borgert-Spaniol, Megan. *Bighorn Sheep*. Bellwether Media. 2014.

Gagne, Tammy. *Bighorn Sheep*. Focus Readers. 2017.

Gish, Melissa. *Bighorn Sheep*. Creative Paperbacks, 2016.

Websites

Canadian Geographic: Animal Facts Bighorn Sheep
https://www.canadiangeographic.ca/article/animal-facts-bighorn-sheep

DK Find Out: Bighorn Sheep Facts
https://www.dkfindout.com/us/animals-and-nature/cattle/bighorn-sheep/

INDEX